PACIFIC

WALL

JEAN-FRANÇOIS

LYOTARD

Foreword

At the end of this short volume baffled readers will discover commentaries relating to a text called *Pacific Wall*, a text I sent Michel Vachey along with a letter dated July, 1974. I am grateful to Michel Vachey* for permission to publish these commentaries (and the text just mentioned) preceded by explanations regarding the circumstances of my discovery. Taken from the same letter, my remarks go like this.

"…In the course of my stay in San Diego one of my colleagues at UC, Mike Vaugham (with whom I shared an understanding of paradoxes inherent in my position as a Parisian invited to be Visiting Professor on the southwest edge of the continent of North America) told me of discovering and paging through a small notebook in the University foreign ms. acquisitions (where he was searching out documents on the Spanish-American War). Roughly forty pages in length, the notebook (in French) had to do—among other things— with this same situation—being a non-resident alien.

At the time Michel Vachey was finishing a ms. with the American language title Toil: *this is a work later (1975) brought out by French publisher Christian Bourgois, preceded by the first edition of* Pacific Wall.

As he seemed to recall, the ms. was signed by a Noushog or Fuckeg or Vachez. Two days later at my request, he took me to the library office where an employee located the ms. call number without difficulty.

"Think of it, dear Vachey, a huge diamond of concrete and plate glass, a glass-faced octagon, erected on hills overlooking the sea and standing in a eucalyptus grove. Ten or eleven floors of it, books and documents shelved on ribs encircling the building's spinal column, with elevators and service pipes inside. As you get off the elevator and walk by the stacks, there are walls of glass sticking out along the way. You also find small tables for diligent readers—and for those less diligent, oversize chairs. Positioned behind the western face of this glass structure, with your feet against the wall, beyond the trees you see a swell of bluish water veiled in mist— the ocean. In the east is a dazzling view of flatlands that can't be seen from above. Beyond, the dull gleam of the first range of coastal mountains. And beyond that, desert.

"You'll find material here for endless labyrinthine searches in your capacity as librarian and archivist— because this completely transparent jewel isn't without paradoxes all the same. It has internal transparency— since every aspect of the culture is available without problem or hindrance because of the extensiveness of the collection and the quality of its classifying system. And it has external transparency too, given its continuous communication with everything nature offers in California—elements, minerals, flora, everything that moves. Though similarly, it's a maze. No sooner is the eye caught in a book's plot or tangle of landscape lines than it begins to jump from one to the other, and the suspicion arises you've been had. And that getting either in or out is impossible for the precise reason that there is no in or out. There's no ground to take hold of and no ground even for taking hold. On the contrary the transparency becomes still more intractable because the specialness of your interest in this book or that view traces new passages in this web of words and things. You're adding something to the labyrinth—though *what* exactly, I can't say.

"And there, turning towards the Pacific, I ciphered out Vachez's manuscript. I'm not certain of the spelling of the name on the first page. The last letter is written badly enough to be either a y or r or z. The inept handwriting made me guess when reading certain parts. To get a working and readable text I went as much as possible on semantic consistency. A demanding job! Because, as you'll see, Vachez wasn't particularly distinguished by either clarity of style or coherency of ideas—and the manuscript is little more than a collection of syntactical and lexical approximations, far-fetched metaphors, unexpected linkings, gross errors and misconceptions, and delirious reasonings. I left the text as I found it, simply restoring its readability. Only the name of the book and interspersed headings are mine. Let me add this too—that in the ms., sections marked off with headings as being separate actually are separate in the text—they become short chapters really. Also, I've added a few footnotes.

"Neither the pleasantness of the venue of my discovery nor the author's name-similarity with yours, dear Mike, would have induced me to send you this text if a third detail hadn't struck me as giving it an odd twist. I made inquiries about this Vachez. My colleague hadn't any recollection of him. Consulting Comp Lit Department records (fortunately scanty, due to the department's having been set up in 1968) I made the discovery that Merlin Vachez (apparently correct unless the presumably Latina secretaries gave the spelling a creative twist) had in fact spent an academic year (1972–1973) at UCSD. Not, to be sure, as Assistant Professor, as he claims, but while doing a library internship. Note that his stay in San Diego precedes mine by only a year. Yet he seems to have left no trace of himself except for this forgotten text. None of my colleagues remembered him. I think of him as spending time in the library or going out to explore beaches and deserts. In any case you can't believe him when he claims to be a professor—even an "associate." Still, the Ms. Greenstone he speaks of actually was a student in French and Spanish with the department. I didn't know her, since by the time I got to California she had got her Ph.D. and left to accept a position at a place in Texas. Since it didn't seem appropriate I didn't try to discover the nature of her relations with Vachez.

"Putting closure to this odd story—I ought to leave it to your discretion to catch one final hint that for me makes this discovery of mine all the more surprising. But I can't help telling you what I discovered. As you'll see when you read the notebook, Vachez ventures on some reflections about military ports and in a section whimsically called "axioms" he makes a bad pun on the name Lorient. My investigation of the meager information provided by records turned up a photocopy request, signed by Vachez, seeking reimbursement for travel expenses and indicating he'd lived in Lorient[*] just before the California internship. I never discovered what took him there or whether he went back after the stay in the USA."

---

[*]*Michel Vachey lives in Lorient.*

A Few Axioms

To Marilyn Monroe[*]

A few axioms should be enough:

FIRST GROUP

The white skin of Western women—meaning the most Western of European-descended American women—is absolute West. My name for the situation of this skin today is California.

To desire that skin puts you in the position of Negroes, Indians, and greasy foreigners. Or pimps. In this situation, non-resident European men who happen to actually be from Europe become greasy foreigners and the property of superior white women—defined as the only ones who "get." European-descended American men act as their pimps.

Absolute West is just cities, just irrigated gardens, beaches, deserts—it's like the Near East that way.

---

[*]Marilyn Monroe is a light beige tabby. *Which is a sentence in American, not in French. (This and the dedicatory note belong to the author of this notebook, whereas interpolated headings of the text, as well as the following notes, are the editor's.)*

The city called Lorient—even if it has an eastern name—is a western port.

Absolute West is a military port. (Or is this a corollary of the previous axioms?)

SECOND GROUP

All politics is a desire for Empire, for domination. And every politician is a pimp.

Empire is indefinite expansion. A *limes* or limit to Empire is set, for the time being only, by exhausting your forward flight and your concern for exclusive appropriation.

Capital realizes a Roman idea of imperial expansion.

American presidents are emperors. Washington is Rome. The USA is Italy. And Europe is its Greece.

THIRD GROUP

Some "nations" don't succeed in settling down into the Empire and are put on reservations. They're displaced to border areas or destroyed.

White skin arouses desire in greasy foreigners like an inside calling up an outside. The skin becomes hollowed out, turning into an inside and giving the appearance of depth, and what results is prostitution.

Racism is the jealousy an imperial name feels for names of whatever's different, for names of migratory nations.

It's also a jealousy each of these nations has for its sisters since any jealousy will produce Empire.

European Jews were a nation without territory. And Germans almost the same. Motto of the Final Solution: having been stripped of our political identity and being a community resulting from the single Election of an invisible principle, we Germans will destroy the Jewish faker.

FOURTH GROUP

European Visiting Professors on campus are Greek tutors: slaves, freed slaves, dependents, wards of Rome, mercenaries of an Amerikapital that worries about its border areas.

The Kienholz Story

Then there's the Kienholz story, told me by a girl studying at UCSD when I was there as Associate Prof. Her mother told it to her, a Mrs. Greenstone, a New York widow who'd just visited the Documenta 5 exhibition at Kassel in West Germany (all this was in the summer of 1972). One of her friends had gone with her, the son of a German Jew who emigrated to New York in the '30s. Mother and daughter had a lengthy discussion about the implications of the piece by Kienholz at the exhibit. It was this discussion that continued through other mouths and ears in California before the Pacific Wall. As a result, a strange set of circumstances came to light revealing a scheme—one of the most notable effects of which was to allow odd passages or displacements, in this case a to-and-fro movement with several loops between Europe and the US. Ms. Greenstone recounted how her mother was struck with Kienholz's refusal to show his piece in a hall, instead getting organizers to set up a huge tent in an area away from the Fredericianum* where the Documenta was

---

*After checking—the only explanation for this error seems to be a choice made by the Greenstones or one made by the narrator or else one made by both.

housed. The Fredericianum, a palace built to honor Frederick II at the time of Prussia's annexation of the Electorate of Hesse-Kassel, was one of the rare old structures still standing after the 1944 bombings. If the heavy tent of dark green canvas, with lighting independent of daylight illumination, wasn't a trap for visitors, then at least it turned out to be an impasse— since you were required to go out the same way you got in. As big as a circus tent, this dead-end was just as moveable. The crime it concealed could be set up anywhere. So that in a short time its moveable nature made it an act of revenge on an imperial American Roman Germanic name by wandering nations. This totally contradicted its contents—a tableau representing a "final solution" of the Negro (migratory) question. But why should this space be arranged as an impasse?

After discussing it, we decided you weren't *supposed* to get through. To go through (going in and out of an exhibition's hallways) would mean due attention to the works displayed. But here that wasn't possible. Turning the corner through an ordinary door along a hallway where thousands of kitsch items were displayed, you entered a place dark even at mid-day—but whose gravel floor all the same showed you'd exited the museum. A

Kienholz's construction was set up at the Neue Galerie, a building constructed after the War with a view of the park area around the Fredericianum, an area referred to as the Schoene Aussicht.

luminous area in back of the tent caught your eye and some of the visitors were clustered there. Others were whispering in the shadows, at first coming in, then going out. So you tried to get closer to the scene to make it out. When you did find out it was too late— since you were part of it now. The light from the rear came from converging headlights of a number of cars stopped in a circle. In the poorly lit periphery, some of the visitors moved slowly, trying not to make noise, while others seemed totally paralyzed. Among them, you were startled at first by a man in shirtsleeves with an immobile face, a face, as you soon realized, that was just a mask. The man in shirtsleeves was leaning on an open door of a pick-up truck—and under his arm was a rifle. Your surprise wasn't less as you noted a woman sitting there in the cab of the same vehicle, throwing up in slow-motion into a scarf held to her mouth. There was also a boy about ten. The glasses he wore made him seem like a precocious school kid—fascinated by the perversity, guardedly staring out at the scene from behind a dusty car windshield.

But you couldn't misunderstand the clothed plastic sculptures Kienholz placed at the convergent point of your vision and the headlights: the three men who held the Negro spread-eagled and the fourth concentrating on cutting off the black man's cock couldn't even for a second be taken for real. Their immobility went beyond what's seen in ordinary tableaus because, declining to continue the deception, where a victim's belly would be expected, Kienholz placed a rectangular pan, a pan in whose black water individual letters floated, letters (read American English here) *which should occasionally drift into position to spell out N-I-G-G-E-R*. The liquid was fed by nothing less than the man's black cock trussed up like a terrifying faucet by the left hand of the castrator, who with his right hand sank in a knife. The shank—*la tige*—of the penis was made out of a piece of ¾" steel shaft—*d'un tube d'acier d'1,905 cm*—which was then welded on the leg frame and which *devait être assez solide pour résister aux* attacks by vandals or souvenir hunters. For Mrs. Greenstone and her friend, the letters swirling in the stream of liquid falling into the pan seemed to evoke some elusive feeling about black nationhood, a thing white imperialism in the tableau was unsuccessfully trying to eradicate. I have to write American here to say *that actually there is no Black man. If you study the piece you will see that what appears to be the victim is, in reality, the three separate White figures (each with part of the black body) shoved up against a central "pan body" which was welded from steel in a human torso form.* And from the fact that even under torture that nation's cock and belly wouldn't give up feeding themselves this nation's independence can be shown. The paradox of the composition is that mobility belongs to the victim even if bound and held to the ground like a pig for slaughter—while what was made immobile around that victim is related to the production of terror. The deception was enough to make visitors halt quickly in fright before that hallucination. From the sheer fact of the sculpture's immobility, you'd tend to confuse yourself with these KKK figures—figures Kienholz sculpted as stupidly intent on imposing an identification onto a liquid belly.

This is the point at which the construction starts up its trick effects. Mrs. Greenstone told her daughter she and her friend began to watch the mostly German visitors as they became enmeshed in the web of Kienholz's weaving. They imagined, instead of the six letters swirling around in the water of the pan, that there were four different ones making the word JUDE. And that Klan disguises were replaced by SS uniforms. They looked on the visitors as monsters, carefully monitoring their reactions, secretly watching their emotions—visitors like the well-dressed mother who gathered her children together quickly and pulled them to the exit so they wouldn't understand the horror. Or like the young couple who just stood there looking dazed. Or the old man they suspected of feigning attention to better conceal a Nazi past. In their minds, whoever approached was guilty. Each had the tell-tale mark of crime laid bare, a crime that spread continuously from the scene in question to visitors through the intermediary of a history that wasn't just a history of the destruction of American blacks or even European Jews but was as well the history of an Empire that could be victorious over itself only at the price of destroying all those partial drives known as minorities. So this next has to be in American too: that mostly *I think of "Five Car Stud," this composition's title, as symbolic of minority strivings in the world today.* Meaning provinces, subdued nations, greasy foreign trash, slaves, free cities. A history of a Caesarean West.

So what were our friends doing when they cast their suspicions on these visitors?! Weren't they themselves involved in the perpetuation of imperialist delirium? It's now they who, at the heart of a new but continuing Empire, expel the Germans around them from the Empire, thus relegating them to a status of a minority contained at its borders. They perfect Western Caesarism at the very moment they feel indignant at its racism, at the very moment they discover it everywhere. They've reinstalled a repulsive whiteness. I never knew Mrs. Greenstone, but her daughter's skin (under lighting conditions of any kind; exposure to the southern California sun gave it only a yet more golden-gray, downy sheen) and a physical presence as devoid of awkwardness as it was of generosity quite clearly consigned her to a fate allotted to white women. It's notable that the figure appearing to be vomiting in the cab of the truck stopped by the whites' cars was a figure of a white woman in whose company the black castration victim supposedly was seen drinking a beer. This bit of information provided by Kienholz seemed important to us—since it's always a Center that arouses a periphery's jealousy. Which is what those shady manipulators called politicians make their business. Under the guidance of the politicians, uppity white skin hanging out with greasy foreigners or black men is considered to be degraded. And the fact that a greasy foreigner's or black man's lust can only be expressed as the obsession to violate white skin means that for the Center you're just a goon or wetback.

On White Skin

"With the exception of human skin, Jarry, nothing has the whiteness or blankness of the furry animals of winter." And so it results that on the blank of human skin there can't be shadows, there can't be relief. Composed of tissue equal to itself at all points, more than any other skin except certain blue-black ones, this skin makes it apparent that bodies aren't volumes, that only surfaces exist. So that that skin is impenetrable. Now the idea of rape is that you penetrate the impenetrable and, at a place infolded by nothingness, you create volume. What's only flatness is forced to become structure, echo like an echo chamber. The epidermal screen has to be invaginated so it becomes a dark receptacle clamoring around the penis—which is what's demanded by jealousy. The denizens of raggedy outlying regions invade and thus constitute the metropolis. Or at least constitute its soft permeability. And conversely, the innocence of a central white blackens whatever desires its blankness.

By castrating a black man, Kienholz's whites want to restore a surface to a monstrous innocence. With their suspicion of the Germans at the Fredericianum* Mrs.

---

*Neue Galerie

Greenstone and her friend do likewise. If your dick happens to be black, you don't exist. Only white has existence. And white's a woman. To the eye and to the sense of touch, the skin at the junction of a white woman's thighs seems comparable in delicacy to a bend of the arm or ankle or nape of the neck.

The consoling thought that a woman doesn't have a sex develops from this. But actually, as a power to inflame, she's all sex. White girls act amazed if as sometimes happens swarthy eyes and fingers make bold to slip off panties or feel dampened furrows that white girls reject as a special site of the act of pleasure. As surfaces, it's not necessary that their bodies even offer themselves, since that would imply a complementary withdrawal—and thus a density.

Complaining that this turns sight to touch becomes possible only if you think of touch as an impact at a single point. But there exists a sweeping movement that simultaneously obliterates and arouses both the person who touches and the one who's touched, effectively transforming both in the same way that an act of looking changes—and exchanges—bodies that see and bodies that are seen. An alteration takes place when, exposed to the great white skies of the California beaches and deserts, part of you gets tanned and the rest stays pale. This develops from the power of tactility. Experiences of this kind leave you dazed. The important thing about touching isn't the establishing of a relation. It's being able to stimulate and provoke intensity or not. How to describe the lust for violation that rouses a greasy foreign dick? It's a paradoxical sense of touch, a sense of innerness whose approximate model would be vaginal touch, would be, I mean, except that a vaginal sense of touch (and this is its justification) aids in maintaining or restoring an organism's health and its silence. In contrast, violating touch seeks (through excitation) to bring the organism into existence so its security is destroyed. Put two or three fingers in your partner's mouth. This stops being a trivial allusion to fellatio and instead suggests some sort of dental or laryngological exam. You're touching a partner's interior or innerness. Say that this touch hasn't any function, that there's no pretext of seeking information, that touch wants to destroy an intrepidity of surfaces, open up depth, destroy sufficiency, make echoes. That's what the lust of someone who's greasy foreign trash is like.

And that lust isn't unfamiliar with a revenge spirit— which is what keeps it weak and in relation to ruling power. Ms. Greenstone and I used to think about Greek preceptors summoned to Roman Italy, about their dreams of vengeance, their determination to violate the intact skin of offspring of the patrician class, hollow out vertiginous depths there. Migrant and immigrant thus find they're endowed with a false glamour, are made deep, or profound. Darkness, subtlety, mobility, naturalization, penetration, and disguises become the fate that's yours as greasy foreign trash. The body cleft in two. As opposed to intact beaches.

In the metamorphosis undergone by someone who's greasy foreign trash, you don't even recognize your own vindictiveness and desire to violate. Rome makes foreign trash like that. The white Caesaress incites masks at her periphery—she sees to it that thicknesses arise. And round and about her are found signs, apish imitators, negroes, greeks, jews, arabs, chicanos, dagos. All of them dark. By making them lust after her, she constitutes their natures as depth. And in having them castrated she affirms the smoothness of her own surface right down to the last fraction of an inch. White women don't have a sex. They take—instead of giving— something. Instead of giving an emotion. Their sensuality's independent of touch. They're inviolable. In the arms of their slaves, spasms racking them haven't an echo or repercussion. Can anything but their own skins make them come? Rape would give this vexed problem the relief of a last word brought into being by first penetration.

Associate Professors

On the function of culture. Why do Romans want Greeks for educators? They appropriate them but make them greasy foreigners. And what do the preceptors want, the ones who come to Rome, the rhetoricians, philosophers, sophists?

They want an experience of themselves as Negroes. They used to think of themselves as white. Now what they want is a displacement of themselves and of "whiteness." They want Empire displaced and they want to be jealous of it. They want to violate.

They also want to make themselves merchandise. You have to be clear on this. They're greasy foreigners because they speak Latin with a Greek accent. And the product they peddle is words.

What got them into the business? They're exporters, importers, transporters. Economic interest and a need to make money are motivations. But this merchandise is also their passion.

In their servitude you see dependency on superior white skin, on ruling power. They come to Rome because Rome is ruling white power, it's capital or a capital—

and at Rome they find white impotency or real power. The emperors are orientals and barbarians who speak Greek or Illyrian. Rome isn't Rome any more. The USA isn't a country. The name of Rome is Caesar. Not a single state but states. Not a single time but many—Atlantic, Central, Mountain, or Pacific Time. Not just one law but several laws.

So non-power or impotency exist within (the) capital. For that, though, you have to be Greek. You have to have been the center. Greasy foreigners are citizens whom power has transferred someplace else. So they claim.

But this version, if nostalgic, is also remunerative—it's the one Rome would like to have. "Teach us our origins—since you are our past!" A point of view (the) capital would like to promote. Origins is the same as merchandise.

Actually there isn't any past on this white skin. The white woman doesn't have a past.

Nefertiti = Marilyn.

The need for origins is one of the wiles currently practiced by little white girls who, since they whimper when they open their thighs, give Greek guys big hard-ons. Which is all organized by the FBI. This is what keeps business going. As culture becomes foreign it becomes, and has to become, critical. Which is to say Greek preceptors become older, wiser, original, and are called on to *paideutize* the US.

A greasy foreigner is constitutionally critical, since he doesn't have American-Roman citizenship. You Associate Profs! It'd be a serious mistake to think you've come to encourage criticism. Greasy-foreign criticism is a weapon of trusts. It defines outer and inner limits, limits between Roman and non-Roman, between citizen and foreigner.

And you authors out there. The upshot of your worries about combining words is only to reinforce borders. At the very most what you succeed in is a greasy "foreignifying" of a few citizens. They used to be pimps and now they're customers. An advantage? Real power is someplace else.

Instead, your purpose in coming here should be to lose your culture, to deculturate. You're not really original Negroes or nomads from antiquity. The nomad character inflicted on you is just a pose, a nomadism of border-dwellers, a form of settling down demanded by Empire. Power on the other hand is still white and "central," not marginal.

It's precisely—to use the American phrase—off limits. Look: this center is the true nomad. The center is actually migratory because all cultures come here and exchange their movement quantities—lose themselves. So come. Come and pillage that migratory movement. Come and carry off its real power. Act like white women. Pretend to be white skin.

The Labyrinth at the Center

There's a necessity causing untainted spaces to regress westward. The imperial *limes* stretches East, but the metropolis never stops moving West. We chatted about Kassel on the shores of southern California. Which is absolute West. Or the enabling mechanism of American capitalism—in other words, Roman power. This is the beauty of the bodies you see jogging on the beaches, in the hills, morning and night, soft headbands holding back the morbidezza of infinite green-blonde hair. It's also the emphasis put on discussion, credited by sunlight. In other words the Greece of stadiums and schools. And it's urban gardens between water and the desert. In other words Phoenicia. It's the desire to try out new phrases, new words, new syntaxes. In other words the Anglo-American freedom of doing business and traveling. Absolute West is an island inhabited by colonists from regions farther east—a place where everything brought in from mother cultures is taken up to effect an emancipation from them. An island of forgetting. Time was when people like Ben Franklin prayed in Philadelphia's Independence Hall for God to rid them of the English tutelage. Today it's West Coasters who slough off an older New England culture. The population of this island doesn't and can't constitute a people. When a culture starts to coagulate as the spirit of a people, as a real country, as anything resembling an organic bond between people and their institutions, this island ceases to be West—and its population becomes indigenous, peasant, rooted, European. We wait for a fragment to be detached, then push farther west, then reconstitute the white blank of surfaces devoid of disturbing feelings, devoid of any localization in a (particular) place. Even paganism would be foreign, as would anything that creates a sense of home— even a religion of peasants.

This place isn't either utopia or an exile, though. This always-displaced serenity is always central—not because it's circumscribed, but because, without coordinates, it acts as a time of origins, in reference to which you locate yourself. If, however, it's itself locatable, if its name comes to be used to designate a feature of some kind, it loses appeal—and another has to be discovered. By calculating from the most recent of these, earlier ones can be extrapolated. It's the capital farthest west, daughter of ones preceding it. So that retrospectively it engenders them, installing them in a narrative, the narrative of western history. This narrative recounts white Empire's expansion eastward. But that East is always only an abandoned West, an ex-center acting as a landmark or darkened whiteness. So that imperial expansion, which is power, only develops reactively, through a base return to origins. And potency—or real power—goes West. About that, make no mistake.

For at the impossible center of Empire (a center that's not a center but instead one of the foci of an ellipse that keeps stretching westward) there isn't a supreme authority. There's a joining up of surfaces—white, ephemeral, labyrinthine, useless. Rome isn't a locatable space in spite of what it owns. Los Angeles is capital of the world because it isn't a European or East Coast-type city. It's not a city with an appearance of unity around some ecclesiastical, administrative, or economic center. It's a checkers game, along whose highways and 40-mile-long boulevards squares are marked off that can always only temporarily be occupied—just like in games. This checkerboard isn't a heraldic female body (including orifices) but a skin that, being white woman, is strict and aleatory contiguousness.

The blank white of this woman skin is light—since all colors (cultures) are mixed together there. The blindness of cars in the maze of streets that's LA is nothing other than a sightlessness of derelicts feeling their way along expanses of hips, shoulders, and groins. The white body isn't an organism. Headless and sexless, can it claim it's a sex and a head, a capital city and a cold act of love, capital? That's what it is, in a sense—just as only in certain ways is a body a unity, an entity, and only in certain ways does it belong to this or that sex: if it's located through a set of coordinates. LA, in contrast, shows what was lost to more ancient capitals one after the other through choice or through fated acceptance of legitimation—namely, that the location of a capital can't be located, that it hasn't a center, and that at the center of Empire there's a migratory white belly. So that the location of the agitated pan that is LA must be continuously replotted.

The Greeks and their doxographers have a story about the fox-fish and its tricks. "It deploys its inner organs, turning them out and sloughing off its body like a shirt." A white woman, a scholar, makes an annotation to the effect that this practice is the same as the one attributed to Hermes in the Homeric Hymn when, stealing Apollo's herd of cows, Hermes puts on trick sandals and makes the animals walk backwards with him, moving from the soft ground to rocks so as to erase whatever tracks were made. And so the god and his silenii, ready to pursue, swirl around in the aporia. A labyrinth isn't some complicated construction where you get lost—it's the body's capacity to undo its own apparent voluminousness, to devaginate itself. So what exactly is it occupies the place of the fox-fish's heart when, in the enactment of its trick, all entrails end up outside? Under the hand of the fisherman and pulling back from the greasy foreigner's dick, the prey vanishes. So that hand or cock is left heavy, useless.

Arriving (thinking you're arriving?) in LA from the northeast, or coming in from the south on I-5 by car or on 395, in the middle of flatlands on both sides or in desert you discover turnoff signs for Kennedy Boulevard, 48th Street, or Laurel Avenue. These are the extruded organs of a city in the process of turning itself inside out. The Western deserts are dotted with these weird limbs. From the signs you can't ever tell what localities these streets and avenues belong to. They don't specify the city you want to pull over and temporarily stop at. The exit sign that says 48th takes you to the desert. At the end there's, let's say, a silent canyon being prepared for development, four-lane roads, sidewalks, manholes, water, gas, and electricity conduits, street lights and as far as the eye can see not a soul—that's what 48th Street turns out to be. These empty lots are corollaries of the so-called ghost towns kept intact in the dry air and sun after the miners all left, towns you get to in high desert reaches at sundown, towns that frustrate your hopes of discovering a stopping place. Are they ghost towns because of having been abandoned or in anticipation? In either case you arrive at a white expanse that can't successfully be occupied. Such places bear witness that in the center of whiteness excess desire hovers over time and space, a surplus potency making each point in this continuum undecidable, a surplus rebuffs any attempt to construct coordinates.

As the white bodies running vainly over California skin show you, traveling takes you nowhere here and everything leads to traveling. There's no boundary in the cities keeping flatlands from deserts. European roads today tell you what you're getting to and what you're coming from. The smallest town introduces itself and takes you in. There's such meticulousness in the way things are marked out that in some suburban areas you pass through cities whose signs might be only a few meters apart, or back to back, or even juxtaposed alongside each other if two city limits cross as you're traveling. Space is dominated in such localizations as animal bodies bound for slaughter, as women's bodies undergoing domination in Chinese erotic warfare, and every part has its special destination. That effort at containing central mobility is the same as the effort made by the county or state administration when it lays out paths and pipelines on the white body, marking out places that'll be lived in and names that are supposed to be countries. Does all this domesticating effort leave the belly wild, unconquered? The Roman roadworks, the quivering displacement of the countryside, the slashing through mountains, the whole highway network with its centralizing effect referring great white blankness to a head—has it all (maybe) been completely vain?

A Genealogy of Politics and Sex

This sort of domination is directly engendered from fear produced by the white octopus. Those constantly parting, shifting silky thighs provoke both power and rape—they institute virility in its two respective modes. That is, they institute politics.

Along with greasy foreigners the panderers appear—politicians, prefects, generals, emperors. These stop the dissimulations of the white belly, they survey and allot extruded skin surfaces, organizing, delimiting them. They thus become the complement of a greasy foreign lust. They're its partner. What then is seen is that the nomadism of the nations of the *limes* is the reverse side of desperate centralism. Philip's, Alexander's Greeks; the Gauls of Caesar; Cortes's Indians are defined as and become foreign or Negro, they're "pacified," decimated, humiliated, not because of being dissolute but because white men, by becoming their masters and relegating them to the edges of the Empire, thought they could expel from the Empire the mobility they considered unbearable.

In the complementarity citizens/greasy foreigner trash, what's at issue is white skin. Citizens and white bosses act like pimps for foreigners. In this deal we make available the opening of our women's white thighs to your tongues, your eyes, your commerce, but under certain conditions. Which ones? None other than gender differentiation and a tripartition of roles. After Caesar, femininity is marked out as a gender. Responding to the come-on of being designated as a second, weaker sex, it exhausts itself—pointlessly—in the struggle for power. After Caesar, masculinity polarizes into cops and criminals, power-havers and power seekers, owners and workers, AMA and MAM. And this doubling is tempted by the trap of referring to itself as dialectically unequal with itself, a stupidity in which the major occultation is occulted—that of incomprehensible white skin.

Pimp, whore, customer: these three roles set up their stage, their theatricality, their voluminousness on uninhabitable white surfaces.

Enter the proletariat. Formerly a greasy foreign customer, this proletariat is promised a promotion to citizen-pimp status. A vision of assimilation! Previously you've been sick unfortunates, border dwellers. But now we proffer shelter, protection.

The white masters like to think of themselves as people who give. They set up a business that at the same time possesses women and allows them to come (come all you want, since you're our property), which allows them to occupy the white female center. Still, only that business has power—a power to receive. What occurs is a usurpation of powers, or faking of functions. Every

Caesar's a fake, an impostor. This male more male than the other men, more male than greasy foreigners, is trading in what he thinks of as women, but what is really only a result (himself being another) of auctioning away empty white expanses. Finally he faces the endless and ridiculous job of integrating it all into a social body.

So that, when distributed, the skin provides you with roles. Caesar usurps the power to receive, changing it into the power to give. Greasy migrating proles from border areas learn to defer sexual gratifications and accept substitute nightmare rape fantasies, get promised a menacing inheritance of masculinity. And last, women are invented as objects to be traded back and forth. And this becomes the stakes of all politics. In good times (today) women are placated with promises of power, so thereafter they're caught up in the double impossibility of recognizing themselves either in the objects they've been made to be or in the supposed subjects men have promised them that they'll be. In their status as prostitutes or as madams, in servanthood or mastery, these white women know something about the profound interconnection of dependency and power. Once that interconnection (the fascinating skin I speak of) is occulted, the stage is set for politics to begin.

Do I really have to spell out what's happening in Kienholz's tent? That a white woman's suspected of going for a beer with a black man? That that's how the woman-thing circumvents her pimps and how both she and her supposed accomplice sense (irrespective of what positions they've been assigned, politically) that they express a power that doesn't have anything to do with the ruling power of little white Caesars? That the business of these Kaiser/Kapital/Amerika men is to go ahead and invent dick and that when they see themselves slicing away at this Negro's pubis they're claiming to be exclusive trustees of maleness? That the black pelvis that continues to produce liquidity, which they try to stop, is also, as Kienholz says, the actual source of their allegedly separate bodies as his torturers? For— and this is the first reason—without their victim they're nothing. But mostly the case is that they and their victim together are creations of true power, here designated as white woman. (I have to put it in American, not French): *Actually there is no black man = actually there are no white men.* She's throwing up.

A dark continent. When Freud compares this dark continent to female sexuality, he unwittingly shows he belongs to a world of the Caesars. The continent of intensities is white—it's not an Africa of conquests or location of disturbances compelled to become outerness, relegated, envied, something to be seen as greasy-foreign or feminine. What's truer is—the continent's a central vertigo for Caesarism as for creation of greasy foreigners as for feminism. It's an undecidability of pale deserts and a boundlessness of skins.

36

Once you think the continent's dark, it's already reduced—and you're talking fake talk or white-man talk. Let's displace. Let's not impose the same greasy foreignification procedure on women that the Austrian emperor did on the Jewish doctor. Let's not replace any emperor, even the greasy-foreign Hannibal. Once a foreigner who's considered a greasy foreigner becomes emperor, he becomes a white Caesar. He invents his own greasy foreigners and, simultaneously, the blackness of his women. At a single stroke his empire sets up all the roles. So by saying "the dark continent of feminine sexuality"—like Mrs. Greenstone and her friend—you too will only perpetuate this imperialism. The black pelvis of Kienholz's Negro is white and aroused. And it's woman because of being in and of itself sexual pleasure and power—prior to any male sexuality whatsoever.

Articulations and Ports

White skin is articulations. No woman would be white and white wouldn't be the space I describe—if there weren't a silent play of delicate parts pivoting on each other in that space, if these wrists, these necks, these ankles, these knees, these elbows, these hips, these curves of a back that also are delicate street crossings, airy public squares that are inconsistent at the edges, relationships between cathedrals and colonnades, avenues swallowed by beaches, modestly terraced and curved hills, desert landscapes grafted with long sinusoid freeways—if all these elements weren't parts gently shifting against other parts in innocent and extreme tension. I imagine the flat projection (captured at 1/10 of a second) of Ms. Greenstone's right tarsus as she does her jogging at Del Mar beach, the calcaneum, the cuboid, the astragalus, the three cuneiform bones and the scaphoid, these tiny temporary profiles of tiny empty volumes that get displaced in relation to each other from one readout to another. A geometrician reading them would need lots of patience to unearth an eternal return here. I imagine the billions of accidents made permanent and the thousands of years of amnesia becoming bone and cartilage necessary to develop (but to what end?) this little device and the thousands and thousands of years of arbitrary selection it took so such a device would have as its sole purpose the pleasure it takes in itself between the imperious tension of an Achilles's tendon and the obstinate counterpressure of the gentle sand.

A sheet of articulations connects pieces of white skin to other pieces. Its arthrography, leading me to unhinge this ankle, will unhinge every other ankle too. If the pin's taken out that joins the sole of Ms. Greenstone's right foot with the footprint in which she remains for 1/10 of a second, I next encounter the connecting of a sandy footprint and a tongue of water that a little wave extends towards it, that in turn's articulated by the dazzling immensity of the Pacific, and then my graphics head out to high seas, till the young woman comes back over the hills, still jogging, and till she reaches "town" in the maze of lanes twining among slightly structured wood houses ornamented with bougainvillea. And this is another series of countless articulations, a series of articulations led in this direction by the undoing of the scaphoid and calcaneum, articulations whose series is called a Californian history of the West, although that history is a histology and that series a simultaneity that nonetheless is incomprehensible. In this way every body—no, bodies don't exist—every connection of the tiniest parts of the body, each with the other, now indirectly and unmethodically leads to others. This is whiteness, skin, the West, and white woman.

One evening, on the east coast in a big city not far from Washington DC, Andrea* and I and some American friends entered a large disco patronized Wednesday nights almost exclusively by male and female black homosexuals (the few Whites there were tolerated as exceptions). There we could see how Blacks are white skin. The brilliant nighttime crowd occupying the dance floor as we entered was made up of couples: the crowd, notwithstanding, in perfect, if unintentional, synchronicity with itself. Shoulders, wrists, buttocks, backs, breasts, and flashing knees undulated within the restricted spaces available to each couple, though there were also indistinct felt hats drooping over undulating eyes, blue-black jackets studded with rhinestones, Levis tucked into patent leather boots, puce-colored satin skirts, velvet shorts leading to slender groins and fashionably curved hips, and so on, so that we started to imagine that this utterly midnight-blue crowd whom the flashing stroboscope broke down into immobile snapshots—like my friend's graphed ankle motions as she jogged along the Pacific—represented to perfection the white skin I've described, since it (the crowd) was made up exclusively of always changing conjunctions of thousands of articulations of individual pieces. So that if we wanted to analyze it we wouldn't have gotten to the end, since a coordinate system was missing. There was, though, something better we had to do— and that was to put aside whatever was assigned to

---

*someone I couldn't identity

us by administrative, academic, moral, political, or artistic institutions under the name "body" and allow it all to come apart, be dissolved in white black skin till it became the multiple anonymous units variously being moved around by what Americans call soul music. The name of the black singer who acted as provisional mover of this surging wave was Barry White. In fact you'd have to be infected with the blindness of the panderers called politicians (including critics) not to see that this voice and the enveloping sounds, far from being in control of the dancing surface, were in fact part of it.

This was paganism, right there in Quaker country. What's Empire afraid of? Who does it push back to the edges, only to have constantly return, sweeping through its center? Precisely this skin. Empire fears its center because it isn't a center at all but an undulation of incomprehensible articulations, a labyrinth of vain paths, measureless delights. Which endlessly are thrown out to a periphery. It installs military ports. The whole *limes* is one immense military port, muzzles pointing out to the surging swell.

And what is this force locked in the souls of cannon, in the machinery of ocean-going vessels, on the empty runways of aircraft carriers, in the muffled gyrations of radar? What is it there so ominously, stored in the alignment of fleets waiting in harbors, presenting threat as an exterior? Jealousy of white skin, white innerness. Jealousy becomes Empire, and it appropriates whiteness. This means a large amount of energy is drawn off from this power, immobilized and earmarked for a projection of power in the form of an enemy—a foreign, barbarian force.

A port gives on the sea. It opens home territories and a native clime to the untamed sea. It allows passage, it's composed of divers articulations, it's white woman. But as a military port, it's a pimp and distributes roles (attacker, defender, defended), separating them from each other, constructing a strategic space for relations of force that come along and conceal articulations. This military port looks East with a zealous eye. It creates the East with its gaze. This Orient (a town called "Lorient") is whatever the sights of its gunmuzzles aim at, it's the other side. A great deal of force is tapped in the West this way—so that the Empire's center is set up as ever tilting towards its western border. Let's not forget—Roman emperors spend their lives breaking camp, then striking it again on a *limes* that runs from one border to the next, showing (in spite of themselves) how power resides not in the capital but on a periphery and in militarized ports. Kissinger. Obliged to constantly make new greasy foreigners. But in fact making themselves greasy-foreign, turning to suspect wanderers, released, then recaptured by a white skin they seek to dissipate.

The Final Solution

Nazis squinting at Jews. Ms. Greenstone told me that
in the course of her reading she discovered how Charles
the Bald's psalm book, which is preserved at the Bibli-
otheque Nationale in Paris (lat.1152), was written
before 869 by (quote unquote) a certain Wagham—
according to Charles R. Dodwell. She also told me the
same prince owned a Gospel, now in Darmstadt
(Landesbibliothek, ms. 476) and (quote unquote) deco-
rated by a certain Wagham ("Uaghamus ornavit")
according to the same source.* We started thinking
about the court of the Carolingian, of the manuscripts
left by him to St.Denis Abbey, and from there our
thoughts turned to the practice, so frequent in the art-
ists' workshops of the day, of copying and illustrating
Old as well as New Testament and identifying the
Frankish emperors of the illuminations not just with
the Caesars but with Moses, a practice suggesting that
at stake in establishing this new Empire was nothing
other than the conquering and circumscribing of a new
Israel. Didn't Alcuin give Charlemagne the *nomen*
David and didn't Pope Stephen V write Louis the

---

*Looking into this, I discovered the painter/scribe in question actually was
named Liuthardus.*

Pious—"Thanks be to God for having allowed my eyes to see the second King David"? And didn't another pontiff compare Charles the Bald to Solomon? And wasn't the cathedral of Aachen a new temple of Solomon as far as Alcuin and Notger were concerned?

Andrea would interrupt these flights of fancy, thinking their direction dangerous. Going along with what historians universally believe to be the case is enough by itself to explain the metaphor, she maintained. According to them, if Jewish traditions had power to win over Franks who only recently had been snatched from tribal paganism, this was specifically because of their tribal character, and if the Carolingians tried to discover an ancestor in David, that was because David's way of coming to power set a precedent for them. Andrea's reservations made her friend spell out the implications of these rambling thoughts.

In fact, he said, how can the recurrence of a Biblical model in Carolingian traditions, inscriptions, and painting be explained if not by some "regression" that led these Franks to seek out an existence not just in allegiance to the recognized and visible heir of Caesar, Rome, but also in a unification principle that owed practically nothing to the political traditions of Antiquity, but whose effectiveness, in contrast, depended on an utterly Judaic conviction that a people (from now on known as Frankish) received its existence from the election of that people by God, and by a promise made by the latter establishing them on the Land provided that they honor his law? To quote from Dodwell's English-language text—"After their conversion, the Franks considered themselves to be replacing the former tribes of Israel in God's special care and protection."

Perhaps too the same "regression" (though as the Professor developed the hypothesis resting on the Pacific wall, he more and more energetically disallowed any use of this term), the same turning back towards an Old Testament might explain the birth and diffusion of millenarian movements throughout Germanic countries some six centuries later at the time of the Reformation or even before (on this point see Kautsky and Bloch). But mostly—and this our Associate Professor never gave up on throughout his imaginary circumambulation around the outer layer of Kienholz's scene—this identification of the first "Germans" and the Israelites provided a key—*the* key, he said imprudently—to the monstrous enigma of a Final Solution applied to the so-called Jewish problem by Nazis. And here's how.

Consider the German people, he said. They're still divided today. Frontiers traverse them that aren't any more *theirs* than the frontiers of the Third Reich were—or those of the First. Take a look at this people's history since Charlemagne. Consider how difficult its national unity is, how belated—in fact impossible. Note the immoderation of its ever-excessive claims (Kaiser Wilhelm at Versailles, the Nazi frontiers), but that of its miseries, too (Treaty of Versailles, crises of the twenties and thirties, current separation from itself). Here and there you'll find scattered symptoms of an essential hesitation about the place this people was given to reside in—a hesitation about its destiny. Note the multiplication of dialects and cultures. And the uncertainty about national borders. There's also the absence of any center—Prussia proclaiming a unification too late for this not to be felt everywhere as an encroachment or pretension (the annexations Berlin presented the German nation being considered by that nation as poisoned gifts). And there's the conflict of religions. All of this, still being present, leaves the nation undetermined, makes its Empire flaccid.

And now we come to the anti-Semitic machinery. Andrea had a hard time making American friends, even Jewish ones, understand the impact of that machinery, she said. It was difficult for these Americans to distinguish between the lesser American wars waged on Jewish Americans by WASPs—a war called anti-Semitism by the former—and the great undertaking of pillage and destruction carried out by the SS administration of the camps. This is my argument: what historical explanation, what hypothesis can account for such monstrousness if only rational explanations, motives, economic and social interests, things of that kind, are brought to bear? If on the other hand, disregarding appearances, and trying to understand the insanity of this destruction on its own terms, you imagine the mainspring of racist terror as jealousy, you then make room for it in a history that obviously stops being a history of historians—in the space-time of drives.

If a people can't succeed in satisfying its demands for territorial unity, demands that develop out of not just bourgeois but Western politics, and assuming this territorial unity lets such a people inscribe a legendary continuity on the soil; if in its existence on this stage it sees itself as meeting only rejection—sometimes swelling so as to overflow legitimate limits on every side, sometimes retreating offstage and disappearing—if then this existence, completely unequal to itself, never manages to become identified through special scarifications on a body of land (scarifications we call Monuments), this people will seek out and will find an identity in some space-time other than that of the political history of occupations of the soil. The quest for German narrative is of this type—and it's a quest that's been more or less continuous at least since Romanticism. It was on this "other stage" too that the extermination of the Jews took place—since for the Nazis, for Germans, and for the entire Old World insofar as it's still a peasant world, that non-territorial stage (a stage where meaning and unity are enacted almost totally as discourse) remains Jewish. The Jewish people isn't a political nation. That people's dispersal and its absence of a center, the multiplicity of its dialects spoken here and there, the deep-going differences separating Askenazy and Sephardic Jews (differences Americans aren't aware of), all that is congruent with the principle that this people derives its existence solely from having been grasped by the Word of an absent speaker and from having been *exclusively* grasped—namely, to the exclusion of other communities.

Oh, the familiar jealousy theme! laughed the Greenstone girl and Andrea, quite unimpressed. In fact, yes—their friend insisted. He also maintained that this is proof the time is ripe to write a history of drives, a history more cruel, less exact, but more precise than a history of interests or trivial enthusiasms. Faced with Jewish wandering, not every Empire contains in its backlogs of jealousy a Final Solution. For it to go to this extreme its greasy foreigners (here, Jews) must quietly refuse to allow themselves to be defined as minorities, even oppressed ones. They have to persist in calling themselves a chosen people of the Kingdom, an Elect against which claims of Empire will now seem forever ludicrous. It's possible this Empire also wants to be a Kingdom. Sheer deception. So this strange impulse has to be added to the pot, that the Empire declare itself marked by election and destined to be Kingdom. When Titus ordained the Diaspora, the political idea hadn't come that far yet. This is because Titus wasn't a Christian and Rome didn't yet nurse the terrorist claim of being simultaneously Empire and prefigured Kingdom of the Elect. Final Solutions require a strange conjunction, election and conquest. The Biblical model of election doesn't give you a thing to conquer, only a request to be heard. And you don't receive Empire. The exclusiveness this people would

like to deserve is one of justice, one that doesn't expro-
priate anyone. A possible implication of this exclusivity
is that a people remain forever greasy foreigners.

It seemed to us that Nazism's sole motive was to wipe
out that election and appropriate its advantages for
itself. It wasn't enough just to conquer. They had to
feel destined to conquer by an elective and transcendent
force, the only power to be able to get these humiliated
Franks back on their feet again. The threat of an exclusive promise made to others had to be extirpated so
the narration of an incomparable blood would become
credible. We know the consequences of that deception.*

Merlin Vachez's notebook ends here.

Wrap-Up

" . . . About this text *Wall*, I don't have to explain to
you how impoverished and cumbersome its language
seems to me and how uninspired and painful its philo-
sophical pretensions are. There's no way of letting this
author off the hook on account of innocence or igno-
rance, since it's hard to believe such subject matter,
sensibility, and even turns of phrase don't owe a debt
to the narratives and cut-ups of Butor, not to speak of
your own. I'm inclined to think of him more as talent-
less than as uninformed or inexperienced.

"Could he really have been unaware that if what he
may have considered the inconsequential dreamscapes
of a single solitary person didn't come under the rubric
of literary genre, it at least exemplified an obsessive
formulation that has not only preoccupied Western
thought—but also motivated many of our most notable
acts? I'm referring to the figure of the parallel. To see
modern democracy as an admired or hated double
of Athens or Sparta, as you know, hardly deserves the
name originality. I grant you the notebook's author
takes more interest in Empire than democracy, in war
than commerce, in slavery than equality, in Rome,
finally, than Sparta. And he invokes Greece only as
defeated, as being coaxed by its conqueror to fashion a
culture for it. Still, the figure remains intact . . . .

"If any feature really is his, it's the way his enthusiasm for comparisons brings him to the most unexpected, most unrelated objects. Your cultural tolerance and the refined sense of *Neben** you've given ample indication of will of course lead you to claim that Vachez intends, through extravagance of comparison, to parody, not conceal the tradition I speak of. In my opinion on the contrary, the unexpected aspects of this text derive from a complete absence of tact regarding geographical and historical fact. Can you tell me for instance if anything gives our author permission to mix his California impressions with an outlandish hypothesis on Nazi anti-Semitism—other than mental confusion? He doesn't balk at pushing the effect to a point of pure and simple nonsense. Do you suppose there's any point to be made out of what he calls whiteness when it's said that his whiteness is too black and that, though peripheral, it resides at the center of Empire, that it acts as a system of coordinates for all displacements while remaining sheer mobility . . . ?

"I can already hear the argument you'll certainly make to plead your namesake's cause, my dear Vachey. You'll tell me what's at issue in this California text is another politics (a vexed phrase I'm reluctant to use), another space, time, or logic, another economics, coming back as if from an outside to criticize aspects of the system

---

A German word meaning "to the side"—in both senses. For a while Michel Vachey made it his motto.

called capitalist, since even that outerness is capitalism's creation, as Indians and Blacks are the creation of Whites. But mostly you'll claim that the nature of this politics is such, and its covering its tracks is so scrupulous, its capacity to dissimulate is so great, that this space of proximities, this time of the ever-already, this logic of incompossibles, and this economy lying beyond value, actually inhabit the white reality that imperial powers drill into us. This utopia would console only displaced intellectuals, you'll warn, if information emanating from all points of the homogeneous gridded space didn't oblige all comers, whether from the political right or political left, to assume the traces of an ungriddable space there. Once within that space, all categories, political ends, even the most 'revolutionary,' become impostures. The current process of decadence, you'll conclude, perverts Empire more than revolution subverts it.

"Will I let myself be persuaded? Your argument certainly touches on one of the infrequent ways *Wall* escapes dilapidation. Let me put this another way.

"If there's something in America which ought to strike a European and which certainly does strike him, but whose shock he resists with all his power, it's not 'decadence.' It's a near lack of existence of a State and the vitality of civil society. Instead of American society being made by additions, annexations and legislations plotted by a center, that center from the beginning owed even its existence to a pact concluded among separate wills, and it owes its permanence only to a competition of interests. The incorporation of Indians, Blacks, and Mexicans into the Union of course was done without their consent—though this imperial trait doesn't make Washington a new Rome. Americans are citizens, while in the makeup of almost all Continentals there's something more like subjects.

"Vachez's parallel obliterates this difference. Like so many others, this European provincial residing in the US won't admit he's changed time-spaces. Nor can he admit another history has begun there already—a history in which there's no central authority that's invoked to resolve problems relating to the social bond. Those problems are resolved, rather, by an accessibility to and a competitive reversibility of channels of information. He should have been struck by what once was called civil society there—a civil society that's now a humanity readying itself for the post-industrial age.

"This resistance is even less excusable given that Vachez was resident in southern California—a place where a combination of geographical, historical, and cultural distances, accumulated influences, a grace of skies and environment, together with wealth, have freed Americans more than others from the European past, predisposing them to take on a version of Capitalism that's now pagan, disencumbered of thoughts of legitimation, interested instead in thinking up this or that new plan and in carrying out the effects of it. A mentality that's not particularly political in an imperial sense.

"So you'll ask: what interested you in such a text and motivated you to send it to me then? Because Vachez is so contradictory. For what does Vachez's poorly constructed *Wall* mean if you take this literally? America comes to a halt dumbstruck before an ocean that puts an end to the Western border. The golden dream's accomplished, and people go about enjoying it. Social consensus isn't sought for in the authority of the capital but becomes a displacement westward. The history of States is coming to an end. Something else can be heard at work—something in the silence of what's finished. What's at issue has stopped being an occupation of lands, and, even less, an exploitation of resources. The issue is conquest of this or that kind of knowledge, committing it to memory, making it available, and the usefulness of this knowledge in creating new plans or developments. And isn't the space-time in which they're resident, in which the game's played, isn't that space-time the same as your 'ungriddable space'? Isn't it Vachez's 'white skin'?"

The Lapis Press
589 No. Venice Blvd.
Venice, CA 90291

Publisher
  Sam Francis

Translator
  Bruce Boone

Editorial & Visual Direction
  Robert Shapazian

Designer
  Patrick Dooley

Le mur du pacifique by Jean-François Lyotard

ISBN 0-932499-64-3

Published 1990

Printed in the United States of America

This translation was assisted by a grant from the French Ministry of Culture.

Cover and endpaper photographs by J. Stephen Hicks.

Photographs of *Five Car Stud* courtesy of Ed and Nancy Kienholz. Ed Kienholz, *Five Car Stud* (1971), private collection.

Cityscape photograph by Linda L. Salzman Photography.

Excerpts from *Le mur du pacifique*, trans. Pierre Brochet, Nick Royle, and Kathleen Woodward, first appeared in English in *SubStance*, 37/38 (1983): 89–99, guest ed. Kathleen Woodward.